For WBM

All rights reserved. For information about permission to reproduce selections from this book, write to trade.permissions@hmhco.com or to Permissions, Houghton Mifflin Harcourt Publishing Company, 3 Park Avenue, 19th Floor, New York, New York 10016.
www.hmhco.com

The illustrations in this book were done digitally.
The text type was set in Chaloops and Eatwell Chubby.
The display type was set in Eatwell Chubby.

ISBN 978-0-544-93907-3

Manufactured in China
SCP 10 9 8 7 6 5 4 3 2 1
4500647167

What
is chasing Duck?

JAN THOMAS

Let's get **out** of here!

What is chasing Duck and Sheep?

What is
chasing
Squirrel?

Looking for more laughs?

COMING SOON

There's a **PEST** in the Garden!
JAN THOMAS

My Friends Make Me **HAPPY!**
JAN THOMAS

My Toothbrush Is **MISSING**
JAN THOMAS

Get your child ready to read in three simple steps!

1 I READ	Read the book to your child.
2 WE READ	Read the book together.
3 YOU READ	Encourage your child to read the book over and over again.